For all the Allison family, with love and thanks — M.M.

To my Grandad, who encouraged me to draw — H.S.

The baby in this book could be a boy or a girl. We have
talked about the baby as 'him', but if your baby is a
girl you could say 'her' when you read the story.

JANETTA OTTER-BARRY BOOKS

Text copyright © Margaret McAllister 2015
Illustrations copyright © Holly Sterling 2015
The rights of Margaret McAllister and Holly Sterling to be identified respectively
as the author and illustrator of this work have been asserted by them in accordance
with the Copyright, Designs and Patents Act, 1988 (United Kingdom).

First published in Great Britain and in the USA in 2015 by
Frances Lincoln Children's Books, 74-77 White Lion Street, London N1 9PF
www.franceslincoln.com

A CIP catalogue record for this book is available from the British Library.

ISBN 978-1-84780-506-5

Illustrated with watercolour, pencil and 'printed' textures.

Printed in China

3 5 7 9 8 6 4 2

15 things NOT to do with a baby

Margaret McAllister

Illustrated by Holly Sterling

F

FRANCES LINCOLN
CHILDREN'S BOOKS

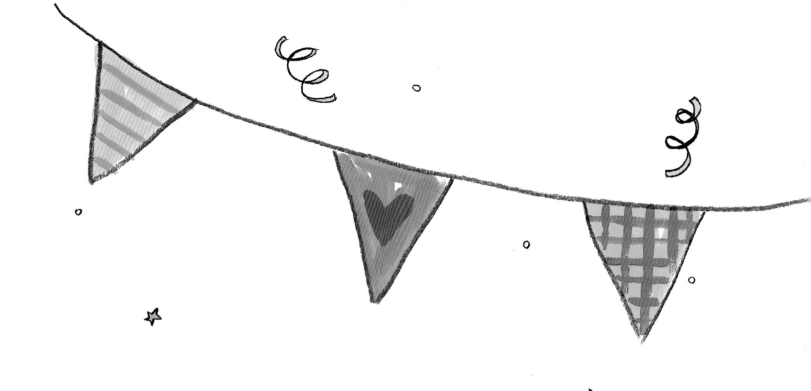

Congratulations!

You now have a baby in your family.

You will make each other very happy,

but you must remember these simple rules.

Don't...

play the **trumpet** when
the baby's trying to sleep,

or send him to play
with an **elephant**.

Don't...

peg the baby on the
washing line,

or send him up in a
hot air balloon.

Don't...

Don't...

give the baby to a
kangaroo,

or wrap him in **brown paper** and post him.

Don't...

plant your baby in the **garden,**

then **forget** where you left him.

Don't...

leave the baby in a
chocolate shop,

or let him help you **paint a picture**.

Don't...

give the baby to an **octopus** to cuddle.

Don't...

take the baby to **school**

or swap him for the school **guinea pig**.

Don't...

let the baby take the
dog for a walk.

Do...

cuddle your baby,

give him a kiss,

sing to him,

make him laugh,

play with your baby,

read to him,

and most of all...

give your baby
lots and lots
of love.